Like Henrietta and Harriet, Penelope Farmer grew up with a twin sister. She started writing at the age of eight and has never stopped since. Her first published stories were written when she was fifteen and were followed a few years later by her first novel for young people, *Summer Birds,* which was runner-up for the Carnegie Medal. Her other stories include *Granny and Me* and *Charlotte Sometimes,* which inspired a popular song of the same name by The Cure. She is also the author of a number of books for adults.

*Henry and Harry were so exactly alike that only their
mother could tell straight off which twin was which.*

TWIN
TROUBLE

Written by
PENELOPE FARMER

Illustrated by
LIZ ROBERTS

WALKER BOOKS
AND SUBSIDIARIES
LONDON • BOSTON • SYDNEY

For Eleanor Ruth Penelope

First published 1996 by Walker Books Ltd
87 Vauxhall Walk, London SE11 5HJ

This edition published 1996

4 6 8 10 9 7 5 3

Text © 1996 Penelope Farmer
Illustrations © 1996 Liz Roberts

This book has been typeset in Plantin Light.

Printed in England by Clays Ltd, St Ives plc

British Library Cataloguing in Publication Data
A catalogue record for this book
is available from the British Library.

ISBN 0-7445-4751-2

CONTENTS

*One morning Harry said, "What's happened, Henry?
You don't look like me any more."*

MUMPS

Their real names were Henrietta and Harriet. But even at school no one called them that. They were called Henry and Harry. Or Henry-or-Harry. Or sometimes just "Twin"; or "Twins".

People called them Henry-or-Harry because Henry and Harry were so exactly alike that only their mother could tell straight off which twin was which. Even she had to look twice sometimes.

The twins had fair hair in bunches, brown eyes and short legs. Harry's feet were just half a size bigger than Henry's. Henry's hair curled a little more than Harry's. At least

Henry said her hair curled a little more than Harry's. Harry said she couldn't see any difference. When they stood side by side and looked at themselves in a mirror, even they could scarcely tell who was who.

"I don't have to look at myself in a mirror to see what I look like, Harry," said Henry.

"Nor don't I," said Harry. "I just have to look at you."

But one morning, Henry woke up not feeling like herself at all. Her head ached. Her face ached. And Harry said, "What's happened, Henry? You don't look like me any more."

"What do you mean I don't look like you?" said Henry.

"You've got a fat face. I haven't got a fat face," said Harry.

Henry got out of bed and looked in the mirror. Harry came and looked in the mirror too. And the faces staring back at them *did* look quite different. Both of them had fair hair still. Both had brown eyes. But Henry had fat red cheeks. And Harry didn't. It felt so strange that they both began to cry.

"What's the matter, *Twins*?" their mother said, hurrying into the room. "Oh dear," she said, as soon as she saw Henry. "Oh dear, oh dear. I'm afraid you've got mumps, Henry."

So that morning, Henry, who didn't look like Harry any more because of the mumps, stayed at home with Mum and baby James. And Harry went to school all by herself.

Harry didn't like going to school by herself, not one bit. Nobody called her Henry all day. They knew she was Harry, because Henry was at home with mumps. She couldn't tease Miss Jenkins, the teacher, by pretending she was Henry, while Henry pretended she was Harry, the way they often did. She was just one person, just like everybody else. Just Harry.

And when she came home there was Henry having a lovely time, tucked up in bed with her favourite story tapes to listen to, and her favourite picture book and her teddy bear, Basket.

"I wish I could get mumps too," Harry said. But she didn't get mumps, not the next day or the next. Though she kept on hoping she would.

Then something happened that made her change her mind. One day there was a new girl in Harry's class. The new girl's name was Susie.

At playtime, when Susie and Harry were playing together on the climbing frame, Susie said to Harry, "Harry's a funny name for a girl. It's a boy's name."

"It's short for Harriet," said Harry.

At playtime, Susie and Harry played together on the climbing frame.

"*Harriet*'s a girl's name."

"Well, then, Harry," said Susie, "would you like to be my best friend?"

"Yes, *please*," said Harry. And after that she stopped wanting to get mumps and stay at home with Henry.

Of course Susie wasn't Harry's first friend. But she was the first friend she hadn't shared with Henry. The first one who'd never had to ask, "Which one are you? Henry or Harry?"

Because Harry went to school by herself now, Susie always knew she was Harry, not Henry. When Harry went to tea with her one day, Susie said to her little brother, "This is my friend, Harry," not "Henry-or-Harry."

Harry still missed Henry going to school with her. But she did like having a friend all to herself. What would happen when Henry went back to school with her? she wondered.

Would Henry find a friend all of her own?

"I'm glad we look just the same again, Harry," said Henry when she was better and they looked at themselves in the mirror again.

"So do I," said Harry. Thinking of her friend Susie, she added, smiling, "But sometimes it's nice just looking like me."

Thomas came up to Henry at playtime and said,
"Harry's got a best friend now."

HENRY'S FRIEND

The day Henry went back to school after having mumps, an unkind boy called Thomas came up to her at playtime and said, "Harry's got a best friend now. Her name's Susie. I don't expect she'll want to be your best friend too."

"I shall always call you horrible Thomas now," said Henry, scowling.

At that moment Susie and Harry came running over.

"I'll never know which is you now, Harry," Susie said, looking upset. "Henry looks exactly the same as you."

"Of course she does, silly," said Henry.

"We're twins. Didn't Harry tell you?" And she marched to the other side of the playground, crossly.

But after school Henry said to Harry, "*I'm* you're best friend, Harry. How can Susie be your best friend too?"

"You're my twin," said Harry, "not my friend. And anyway, why can't I have two best friends?"

But Henry didn't want Harry to have two best friends. Next day, when Harry wasn't looking, she went over to Susie and pretended to be Harry. "Do you want to share my bag of crisps?" she said. "I'll share them with you because you are my best friend."

Susie thought Henry really was Harry at first. She started to say, "Yes please, Harry." But at that moment the real Harry appeared. At once Susie pretended she hadn't mixed

16

her up with Henry. She glared at Henry and said to Harry, "Let's go and play in the Wendy House, Harry. You are my best friend, not Henry."

And then Henry stood in the corner of the classroom all by herself, feeling sad.

When they got home that day, Henry was nasty to Harry. She kicked her. She emptied all her crayons onto the bedroom floor. In the bath she splashed Harry right in the face.

"What's got into you, Henry?" Mum said, looking anxious. "Perhaps you're not really better from mumps."

But Henry was better from mumps. She was just angry with Harry.

And now Harry, too, felt sad. She offered to give Henry her best paintbrush. She said she could colour the nicest picture in her colouring book. She promised to let Henry use their favourite teddy-bear plate at teatime.

But Henry didn't want the teddy-bear plate. She didn't want to colour in Harry's nicest picture. She threw Harry's best paintbrush on the floor. She was so angry with Harry she didn't even want to eat her tea. She only wanted Harry not to be best friends with Susie.

Harry said, still more sadly, "But Susie is my best friend. You'll have to find your own best friend, Henry."

"Don't want to," said Henry. "You're my best friend, Harry."

Next day at school, horrible Thomas came over to Henry. He didn't have a best friend either. He said, "Tell you what, Henry. I'll be your best friend, if you like."

"All right," said Henry. But she didn't care. Horrible Thomas was still horrible, she thought. But if Susie was Harry's best friend, she'd better have a best friend too; even a friend like horrible Thomas.

At playtime, Thomas showed Henry his Action Man. Susie and Harry were playing a skipping game. Henry thought Action Man was much more fun than skipping games.

And then at dinnertime Thomas let Henry have half his chocolate yogurt while she had half his strawberry yogurt. And he let Henry take off Action Man's soldier suit and put on his football outfit instead. Perhaps being best friends with Thomas wouldn't be so bad after all, Henry thought.

At home that evening Harry offered to lend Henry her best paintbrush *and* her favourite story tape. Henry smiled and said, "Yes, please, Harry."

And she ate a very big tea – three fish fingers, two cupcakes and a banana.

"Now I know you really *are* better from

mumps, Henry," said Mum.

Harry said, "Now Henry's quite better, can Susie come to tea?"

"And can Thomas come, too?" asked Henry. "Thomas is *my* best friend," she added.

*Thomas and Henry both practised pulling an ear
till Miss Jenkins rang the bell.*

Secret Signals

So now Harry's best friend was Susie and Henry's best friend was Thomas. The only problem was the twins still looked exactly the same. And Susie and Thomas couldn't always tell who was who.

One dinnertime, for instance, Thomas went up to Harry and said, "Hullo, Henry."

"How can you be my best friend," said Henry, "if you can't even tell she's Harry and I'm Henry?"

Another day, Susie went over to Henry and said, "Hullo, Harry."

"I'm Harry," said Harry, crossly. "She's Henry. How can you be my best friend,

Susie, when you don't even know whether I'm Harry or Henry?"

Henry and Harry began trying to think of some way for Thomas and Susie to tell which twin was Henry and which was Harry. Thomas and Susie began thinking too. Next day Thomas came over to Henry and said, "You are Henry, aren't you, Henry?"

"Yes," said Henry.

"Well, I've got an idea," said Thomas. "And my idea is we can have a secret signal. If I make the secret signal, and you make it back, then I'll know you're Henry, not Harry. And if you don't make it, I'll know you're Harry, not Henry."

Henry liked the idea of having a secret signal. Susie would still go on getting Henry and Harry muddled up. But Thomas wouldn't.

"What sort of secret signal?" Henry asked.

Thomas thought a bit more. "Suppose you pull your ear, Henry," he said at last. "Then I'll know it's you. If you don't, I'll know you're Harry."

"All right," said Henry. And they both practised pulling an ear till Miss Jenkins rang the bell and they had to go back into the class.

It was Science that afternoon. Their class were learning which kinds of things would float in a basin of water and which wouldn't. Thomas kept pulling his ear. Henry kept pulling hers. They didn't pay much attention to Miss Jenkins. When Henry had to drop a piece of metal in the water to see if it floated, she dropped it so carelessly, Susie and Harry got splashed. Henry and Thomas laughed and laughed. Miss Jenkins was cross.

"Why do you keep pulling your ear, Henry?"

said Harry, that evening. But Henry didn't answer. She wasn't going to tell Harry she was practising her secret signal. It was the first secret she hadn't shared with Harry.

But she couldn't keep a secret from Harry for long.

Next day Harry asked again, "Why do you keep pulling your ear, Henry?"

And this time Henry said, "I'm practising my secret signal. So that Thomas will know I'm me and not you."

"Perhaps Susie and me could have a secret signal too," said Harry.

"What sort of signal?" said Henry.

Harry thought. "I know," she said. "I'll tap my nose. And then Susie will always know it's me, not you, she's talking to."

At breakfast, Henry practised pulling her ear, and Harry practised tapping her nose. They almost forgot to eat their breakfast.

They made baby James laugh in his high chair. They were very nearly late for school.

"Twins," sighed Mum.

But from that day on, Thomas knew that the twin who pulled her ear was Henry. And Susie knew that the twin who tapped her nose was Harry. They were the only people, along with Mum, who didn't get Henry and Harry muddled up.

Henry crept up behind Tracy and snatched the doll from her.

TWIN TROUBLE

One day Henry went to school in a naughty mood. She pulled Susie's hair. She wrote her name on Harry's book. She made a face at the playground lady when her back was turned. She was cheeky to the dinner lady. Henry feeling naughty made Harry feel naughty too. She, too, made a face at the playground lady. She, too, was cheeky to the dinner lady. She, too, scribbled all over her drawing-paper instead of making a proper drawing.

"Twins," sighed Miss Jenkins. "I don't know what's got into Henry-or-Harry today, I really don't."

All the same it wasn't Henry-or-Harry who did the very naughty thing. And it certainly wasn't Harry who did it. It was Henry.

Tracy Potter had brought to school the new baby doll that her granny had given her for her birthday. When they went back into the class room after dinner, she let all the girls in the class hold it – and the boys, too, if they wanted. The baby wore a flowered pink dress and a flowered pink hat. It looked very pretty. But because Henry was feeling so naughty, she didn't want to wait for her turn to hold the doll. She crept up behind Tracy and snatched the doll from her. She snatched it so roughly, she tore off the ribbon that held on the doll's pretty pink hat. And then she made things worse by throwing the doll on the floor.

Tracy Potter began to cry. Miss Jenkins made everyone go back to their seats. She looked sternly at Harry and Henry.

"That was very naughty, Henry," she said. "You've been a naughty girl all day."

But Harry didn't like Henry getting into trouble. "Henry didn't hurt Tracy's doll," she said. "I did. I'm Harry," she added.

"No, Harry didn't," insisted Henry, "I did it. I'm Henry."

Miss Jenkins sighed. "Did any of you see who snatched Tracy's doll?" she asked the rest of the class.

"I thought it was Henry," said Polly Simms.

"I thought it was Harry," said Iqbal Patel.

Miss Jenkins looked at Susie and Thomas. But without the special signals, even they couldn't tell which twin was which. She sighed again, and said, "Then I'll have to take both of you to see Miss Clissold." (Miss Clissold was the head teacher.)

Henry's best friend, horrible Thomas, waved his hand in the air. "That's not fair, Miss," he said. "They weren't both naughty. They didn't both hurt Tracy's doll."

"But they are both being naughty now," said Miss Jenkins. "They are being naughty by not telling me which of them spoilt Tracy's new doll."

Harry and Henry just smiled at each other. They did not want to go and see Miss Clissold. But it would be much easier to go and see her together. And besides, muddling everyone up like this was fun.

Tracy Potter didn't think it was fun, though. She was crying over her doll. And now Henry looked across and saw her crying. And suddenly she didn't feel naughty any longer. She just felt sorry she had spoilt Tracy's new doll. And she thought how cross Mum would be when she found out. She hung her head and looked up at Miss Jenkins.

"I didn't really mean to hurt Tracy's doll," she whispered. "It was me who did it. It wasn't Harry."

Harry saw Tracy crying too. And she felt as bad as Henry. She took her twin's hand. "I'll come with you to see Miss Clissold, Henry, just the same," she whispered.

But because they were sorry, Miss Jenkins didn't take them to see the headmistress, after all. She found a needle and pink thread and sewed the ribbon back on the pink hat of Tracy's doll so neatly you couldn't tell it had ever come off. Even Tracy began to smile again.

"From now on, though," said Miss Jenkins, "we're going to have to think of some way of telling which of you twins is Henry and which Harry, aren't we?"

"Yes," said Henry and Harry, together.

After the twins had hung up their coats in their class cloakroom, they hid behind the end row of pegs.

BUNCHES

Next morning at school Miss Jenkins said, "Now, Henry and Harry. Now, everyone. Who can think of some way of telling Henry from Harry, so that we stop getting them all muddled up?"

"They can wear badges with their names on," suggested Thomas.

Henry and Harry looked at each other and shook their heads. They didn't want to be the only ones in the class with name badges on.

"Why can't Harry always wear a blue jumper and Henry a red one?" asked Susie.

Again Henry and Harry shook their heads. They both liked wearing blue jumpers one day and red the next.

"Well, I've an idea," said Miss Jenkins. "They can wear different coloured bands on their bunches. And then we'll always know which twin is which."

When Mum came to fetch them at home time, Henry and Harry told her all about Miss Jenkins's idea. Mum, too, thought it was a good idea for Henry and Harry to have different coloured bands on their bunches.

"I want red bands on mine," said Henry.

"So do I want red bands on mine," said Harry.

"Well, you can't *both* have red bands," said Mum. "How about you having blue bands, Harry?"

"All right," said Harry.

So it was settled. Everyone in Henry and Harry's class knew that the twin with red bands on her bunches was Henry, that the twin with blue bands on her bunches was Harry. Even Thomas and Susie didn't need their special signals any more to know which twin was their best friend and which twin wasn't.

But one day, Henry said to Harry, "I like being Harry sometimes instead of Henry. I like people muddling us up."

"So do I," said Harry.

"Well, *I've* got a good idea now," said Henry. And she whispered some thing to Harry.

"That's a very good idea. Let's do it tomorrow," Harry whispered back.

Next day, as usual, Mum fixed red bands to Henry's bunches and blue ones to Harry's. But after the twins had hung up their coats in their class cloakroom, they hid behind the end row of pegs and Henry took the red bands off her bunches and put them on Harry's, and Harry took the blue bands off her bunches and tied them onto Henry's.

Then they went into their classroom and sat down in their places. Or rather, Harry, wearing the red bands on bunches that weren't nearly so neat as when Mum had tied them, sat down in Henry's place. And Henry, wearing blue bunches on *her* not-so-neat bunches, sat down in Harry's.

Miss Jenkins got up to read the register.

"Henry," she called. And Henry almost answered "Here", forgetting she was supposed to be Harry today. Harry kicked her. "Here," she said. And when Miss Jenkins called "Harry?" this time Henry remembered she was Harry and shouted, "Here," loudly. And both of them giggled.

"What's got into you twins today?" said Miss Jenkins.

Henry whispered to Harry, "This is *fun*."

There was only one problem. Even though Henry and Harry were twins, they didn't do the same things *all* the time.

They had different reading books, for instance. Henry's was about Pinky the Pirate. Harry's was about a girl called Jemima. Henry knew all the hard words in Pinky the Pirate, but she didn't know all the hard words in Harry's book about Jemima.

"I am disappointed in you today, Harry," said Miss Jenkins. "You'll have to read that page to me all over again."

Miss Jenkins didn't say she was disappointed in Harry, though. Harry did get some of the hard words in Henry's book right. And Miss Jenkins said she could go to the projects table and stick some more prickles on Henry's model of Sonic the Hedgehog.

Harry was pleased. But Henry wasn't. It

was her model, really. She didn't want Harry sticking prickles on Sonic the Hedgehog. Her face went red. She pinched Harry.

"What's the matter with you, Henry?" said Miss Jenkins.

"I want to work on my model, too," said Henry.

"But you can't, Henry. I want you to read to me again," said Miss Jenkins.

At playtime Henry looked out for Thomas, as usual. But then she realized that because she was Harry today, Thomas wasn't her best friend, Susie was. And that if Susie was her best friend, she wasn't going to be able to play with Thomas's Action Man.

Susie had brought her Puppy in my Pocket to school that day. But Henry didn't feel like playing with Puppy in my Pocket. She went up to Thomas and pulled her ear, so that Thomas would know she was really

Henry, even though she was wearing Harry's blue bands. But Thomas only said, "Why are you making Henry's signal, Harry?"

At dinnertime, Henry said, "Shall we change our bands back, Harry? Then you can be Harry again, and I can be Henry."

"Oh no," said Harry. "I'm having a lovely time. Let's stay being each other till going home time."

"All right," said Henry, a little sadly.

They had painting in the afternoon. Henry did a picture of Miss Jenkins. She thought it was one of her best paintings. So did Miss Jenkins. She pinned it up on the wall. She wrote underneath it: "Harry painted a picture of Miss Jenkins." But Henry thought, *Harry didn't paint it; Henry did.*

At playtime Henry found a big black

feather in the playground and gave it to Miss Jenkins to put on the nature table. Miss Jenkins labelled it. "Harry found a crow's feather." But Henry thought, *Harry didn't find it. I did.*

Harry was sorry that Henry was upset. She found a big white pebble and put it on the nature table. Miss Jenkin wrote underneath it: "Henry found this pebble." But Henry didn't want her name under a big white pebble. She wanted it under her big black crow's feather.

At last it was home time. Mum came to meet them with baby James in the pushchair. Henry still had Harry's blue bands on her bunches. Harry still had Henry's red ones. Just the same, Mum knew which of them was Henry and which was Harry.

"How's my Henry?" she asked, giving her a big hug. "And how's my Harry?"

" 'Enry," said James, giving Henry a big smile. " 'Arry," he said, smiling at Harry.

Henry felt happy. Because even if she was still wearing Harry's blue bands, she felt like Henry again.

When Harry said, "It was fun being you all day, Henry," Henry answered, "But I like being me better don't you, Harry?"

And then she said to Mum, "It's Christmas soon and I know what *I* want Father Christmas to bring me. I want an Action Man, just like Thomas's."

"And I want him to bring *me* Puppy in my Pocket," said Harry.

Henry and Harry stood over the crib and sang
"Away in a Manger" all by themselves.

LITTLE ANGELS

Christmas was coming, and Henry and Harry's class were going to do a nativity play. Henry hoped to be one of the Three Kings. Harry wanted to be Mary. But Henry's friend Thomas was chosen to be one of the Three Kings. And Miss Jenkins told them Mary was to be Harry's friend Susie.

"And as for you, Henry and Harry," Miss Jenkins said. "I want you to be my angels in the nativity play, watching over the baby Jesus. It will look so sweet having two angels who look just the same."

But Henry and Harry didn't want to be

angels. It was all right to look the same when they were bridesmaids. Harry and Henry were always being bridesmaids, because everyone said how nice it was to have bridesmaids who looked exactly the same. But in the nativity play they wanted to be different.

"I wanted to be a King," whispered Henry, sadly.

"I wanted to be Mary," whispered Harry.

When they went home that evening, Mum said she was sorry Henry wasn't a King and Harry wasn't Mary.

"But you'll make lovely angels, just the same, Twins," she said. "Angels are very important. And Dad and I will come and see you being angels and we'll clap and clap. Two angels just the same will look very sweet."

Still, Henry and Harry didn't want to look

just the same. But next day when they came home from school, they found Mum had bought lots of gold and silver paper. She was cutting up a white sheet to make their angel robes. She showed Henry and Harry how to trace out feather shapes on white paper and then she helped them cut out the feather shapes, to stick on their wings.

Henry and Harry had forgotten all about angels having wings. The wings Mum was making for them were very big. They looked lovely. Kings didn't have wings. Mary didn't have wings.

Mum made them try their costumes on. When she had fixed the wings to their backs, they went to look at themselves in the mirror. Instead of Henry and Harry, two little angels stared back at them. Of course, they looked exactly the same. Henry still wished, just a little, she could have been a

King, and Harry still wished, just a little, she could have been Mary. But Mum was fixing gold bands and white haloes to their heads now. Looking at their haloes and their wings, Henry and Harry began to think that being angels mightn't be so bad, after all.

And then, next day, Miss Jenkins said Harry and Henry sang so nicely that the twin angels could sing a verse of "Away in a Manger" all by themselves. Henry and Harry were very pleased.

That evening, Henry said to Harry, "Do you know, Harry, I think being an angel is almost as nice as being a King," and Harry said to Henry, "So do I think being an angel is almost as nice as being Mary."

The day of the nativity play came at last. Henry and Harry wore their white robes and their big feather wings decorated with gold and silver. They stood over the crib and sang the verse of "Away in a Manger" all by themselves very nicely. No one looked at the baby Jesus then, or the Three Kings or the shepherds or Mary. They were too busy looking at the two little angels guarding the crib. How sweet it was, they said, having two angels who looked exactly the same.

Mum said she was proud of them. So did Dad.

When they went to bed that night, Henry said to Harry, "I liked being an angel. Sometimes I like looking just like you."

"I liked being an angel, too. Sometimes I like looking just like you, too, Henry," said Harry.

At teatime Mum said, "Have you decided what you're going to wear to your party, Henry and Harry?"

FANCY DRESS

Soon after Christmas came Henry and Harry's birthday.

Everyone in Henry and Harry's class were interested. They'd never known two people to share a birthday before.

"How about a fancy-dress party?" said Mum. "You can invite all your friends."

Henry knew just who she wanted to be at the fancy-dress party. "I'm going to our fancy-dress party as Sonic the Hedgehog," she announced to Mum.

"But I don't want to go to the party as Sonic the Hedgehog," said Harry. "I want to go as Little Bo Peep. Baby James can be one of my sheep."

"Yuk," said Henry. "I don't want to go to the party as Little Bo Peep."

"Nor do I want to go as Sonic the Hedgehog," said Harry.

Next day at school Thomas said to Henry, "I am going to your party as a dinosaur. What are you and Harry going as?"

Susie said, "I am going as Little Miss Muffet. What are you and Henry going as, Harry? How about Jack and Jill?"

All the way home Henry thought about being Sonic the Hedgehog. But she didn't say anything to Mum or Harry. And all the way home Harry thought about being Little Bo Peep. But she didn't say anything to Mum or Henry.

At teatime Mum said, "Have you decided what you're going to wear to your party, Henry and Harry? Dad says he'll help you with your costumes. But he hasn't got much time."

Dad said, "What about going as Hansel and Gretel?"

"Or what about Robin Hood and Maid Marian?" suggested Mum.

Henry looked at Harry and Harry looked at Henry.

Henry said, "But I want to go as Sonic the Hedgehog."

And Harry said, "And I want to go as Little Bo Peep."

"What's wrong with that then?" said Dad. "I think I can manage Sonic the Hedgehog and Bo Peep all right, with a little bit of help from Mum."

"But Sonic the Hedgehog and Bo Peep aren't the same," said Henry.

"You don't have to go as the same thing," said Dad.

*Henry wore a grey-brown suit with prickles all over it,
and Harry wore a big straw hat and a pretty blue dress.*

"But because we're twins and it's our birthday, everyone else thinks we'll go as the same," said Harry.

"Then you've got a secret," said Dad. "No one will guess you're going to be different. How surprised they'll be."

Next time horrible Thomas asked Henry what she and Harry were going to wear to the fancy-dress party, she said, "It's a secret."

And when Susie asked Harry what she and Henry were going to wear, Harry replied, "It's a secret."

And somehow they managed to keep that secret until the party came.

Henry wore a grey-brown suit with prickles all over it and a brown hat and Mum's brown stockings on her hands and feet for paws. And Harry wore a big straw hat and a pretty blue dress and carried a shepherd's crook with a blue bow tied round it. Not for one minute would anyone have thought they were twins.

As for baby James – when Henry showed her Sonic the Hedgehog costume to everyone, she held James by the hand, dressed as a baby Sonic the Hedgehog, and everyone clapped. As soon as she'd finished, she took off his hedgehog suit. And when Harry showed *her* Bo-Peep costume, James trotted after her, wearing the white sheep's costume that been hidden underneath the hedgehog suit. It had a long tail. James kept turning round to try and catch it. Everyone clapped louder still.

Susie and Thomas said to Henry and Harry, "We'd have thought you two would dress up the same, like when you were angels. You are twins, after all."

But Henry and Harry answered, "Just because we're twins doesn't mean we *always* have to be the same."

THE

END

GRANNY AND ME

Penelope Farmer

Ellie loves being with Granny. She likes her bright clothes and the funny un-Grannyish things she does, such as climbing up ladders and painting her face like a tiger. Doing anything with Granny is fun – staying the night, going to playschool or the swings, even dull things like planting cabbages. And when Ellie is cross about her new baby brother, it's Granny who makes her feel better. Share Granny and Ellie's adventures in these six delightful stories.

THE STONE MOUSE

Jenny Nimmo

"The book is written in a direct and unsentimental style that is a pleasure to read. Helen Craig's drawings are finely tuned to the story and beautifully executed." *The Times Educational Supplement*

Jenny Nimmo worked at the BBC for a number of years, ending in a spell as a director/adaptor for *Jackanory*. Her book *The Snow Spider* won the 1986 Smarties Book Prize and, with the other two books in the trilogy, *Emlyn's Moon* and *The Chestnut Soldier*, was made into a popular television series. Among her other titles are *The Owl-tree*, Winner of a Smarties Prize Gold Award (6–8 category), *Ronnie and the Giant Millipede* and *Toby in the Dark*. Jenny Nimmo lives in a converted watermill in Wales with her artist husband and three children.

Helen Craig has illustrated many children's books, including *The Town Mouse and the Country Mouse* (shortlisted for the 1992 Smarties Book Prize) and four *This Is the Bear* books.

MORE WALKER PAPERBACKS
For You to Enjoy